Don't count the
Count how happy y
Bear, and I'll help
the best ever.

cloud on
grouchies

m
av

u;

dreams.
I'm a bit

we hope
that you'll have a special place for us in your
heart, just like we do for you.

With love from all of us,

The Care Bears

This Book Belongs To:

Rachel
Simone

Care Bears, Tenderheart Bear, Friend Bear, Grumpy Bear, Birthday Bear, Cheer Bear, Bedtime Bear, Funshine Bear, Love-a-Lot Bear, Wish Bear and Good Luck Bear are trademarks of American Greetings Corporation.

Library of Congress Cataloging in Publication Data: Ludlow, Margaret, The Trouble With Timothy. SUMMARY: Friend Bear from the land of Care-a-lot shows Timothy that it is not necessary to misbehave in school in order to gain attention and be liked.
[1. School stories   2. Behavior—Fiction   3. Toys—Fiction]   I. Cooke, Tom, ill.
II. Title.   PZ7.L9749Tr 1982 [E] 82-18912   ISBN: 0-910313-00-8
Manufactured in the United States of America.   7 8 9 0

A Tale from the

Care Bears™

The Trouble With Timothy

Story by Margaret Ludlow
Pictures by Tom Cooke

Monday was not a good day.

On Monday, Timothy made a paper airplane out of his arithmetic test. He sailed it across the classroom. It landed in the fish tank.

Mrs. Pratt was angry.

"Who did that?"

Mrs. Pratt pulled the paper airplane out of the fish tank and unfolded it. The paper was wet, but she could still read Timothy's name on it.

"Timothy, I want you to write 'I will not throw things in class' ten times and bring it in tomorrow with your homework."

Timothy spent Monday after school digging for worms in the backyard. That night there was a really good movie on television.

So Timothy forgot to write "I will not throw things in class" ten times. He didn't bring any papers to school on Tuesday.

What Timothy did bring in on Tuesday was a little white box. He put it on Jennifer's desk.

When Jennifer saw the little white box, she was very excited. "Look, somebody gave me a present! I wonder what it is? Maybe it's a ring."

Jennifer opened the box.

"Eek! It's a worm! Oh, yuck. Get it away from me!"

Jennifer leaped out of her seat so fast, she knocked the box off her desk. The worm fell out and slowly crawled across the floor.

All the children started yelling, "Worm! Worm!
Watch out for the worm!"

Mrs. Pratt had to bang on her desk
with a ruler to quiet them down.

"Whose worm is that?" she asked.

"It's Timothy's worm!"
everybody yelled.

Mrs. Pratt sent Timothy to the principal's office.

Wednesday was a terrible day.

When Mrs. Pratt turned to write on the black-
board, Timothy tried to be funny. He stuck out his
tongue, crossed his eyes and made a horrible face.
Before he could stick his tongue back in and uncross
his eyes, Mrs. Pratt turned around. She did not think
he was funny.

When Mrs. Pratt asked, "If I have two apples, and you have two apples, and we put them together, what do we have?" Timothy shouted, "Applesauce!"

When Mrs. Pratt called on him to read, Timothy couldn't find the place in his reader, because he was busy drawing Swamp Monsters in his notebook.

Mrs. Pratt wrote a note to Timothy's parents.

When Timothy's parents read the note, they sent Timothy to his room.

"Nobody likes me," Timothy said to himself. "Everybody hates me. Mrs. Pratt hates me. Jennifer hates me. Even my father and mother are angry with me right now. I don't have a friend in the world."

Timothy sighed and sat down on his bed. Suddenly he noticed that a bear with daisies on its tummy was sitting on his pillow. Timothy was surprised. He picked the bear up.

"What are you doing here? I don't own a bear like you. Are you a present?"

The Bear giggled. "Oh—oh, please stop patting my tummy. It tickles!" Timothy was so amazed to hear a bear speak that he almost dropped it.

"Careful, careful," smiled the bear.

"You *are* talking. I never heard a bear talk before."

"You never needed a friend so badly before. You said that you didn't have a friend in the world."

"That's true," Timothy said sadly.

"No, it's not. I'm your friend, your snuggly, furry friend. In fact, that's my name, Friend Bear, and I come from the land of Care-a-lot. I'll be around as long as you need me, but when you don't need me so much, I'll be on my way. Now, I think I can help you."

"How?" said Timothy.

"The way that I see it, you don't like school very much."

"Why should I?" asked Timothy. "School's no fun."

"But it can be," said Friend Bear. "I'll show you. Let's play a numbers game with your models."

"Can you do numbers?"

"Can I do numbers? Can a rabbit roar? Can a pig fly?"

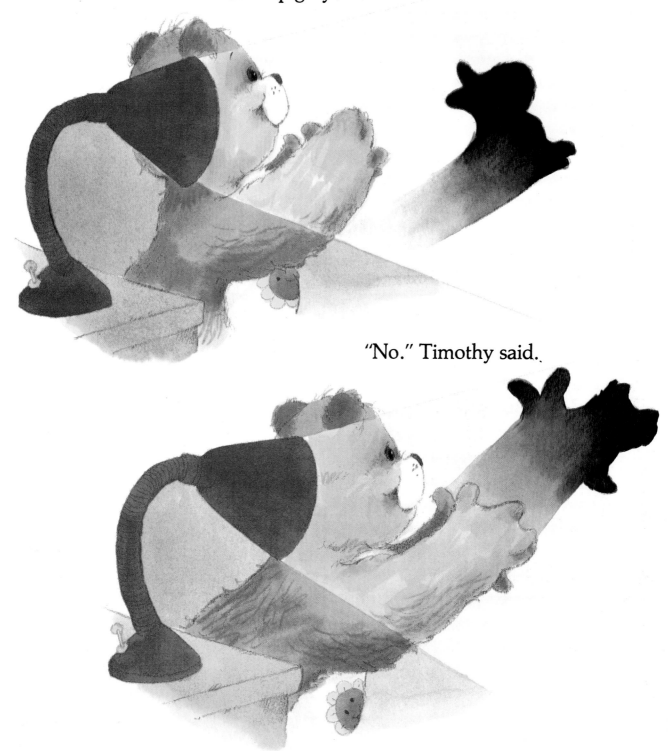

"No." Timothy said.

"Maybe not," said Friend Bear. "But, I can do numbers. Now look. You have one Swamp Monster, one dinosaur and one Snakeman. If I take the dinosaur," Friend Bear took the creature and climbed up on the bed, "how many monsters do you have left?"

"Two," Timothy said.

"Very good! As easy as falling off a log." Friend Bear tumbled off the bed and rolled over to Timothy. "When Mrs. Pratt asks you to do arithmetic, why don't you use your imagination? You don't *always* have to add apples."

"That's a good idea for arithmetic," said Timothy, "But what about reading? I don't like reading. We never get to read about really good things, like rockets or monsters."

"We'll play another game," said Friend Bear. "Do you have a pencil and paper?"

"Of course." Timothy got them out of his desk.

"This is a reading game,"
Friend Bear explained.
    "Can you read?" asked Timothy.
    "Can I read? Can a snake tap dance?

Can a cow roller skate?"
"I doubt it," said Timothy.
"Me too. But I can read."

Friend Bear picked up the pencil and printed something on the paper. "Can you read what it says?"

Timothy looked at the letters. "No, not really."

Friend Bear pointed out the words. "It says, 'Swamp Monsters From Outer Space Meet The Snakeman'. If that were a story in a real book, would you want to read it?"

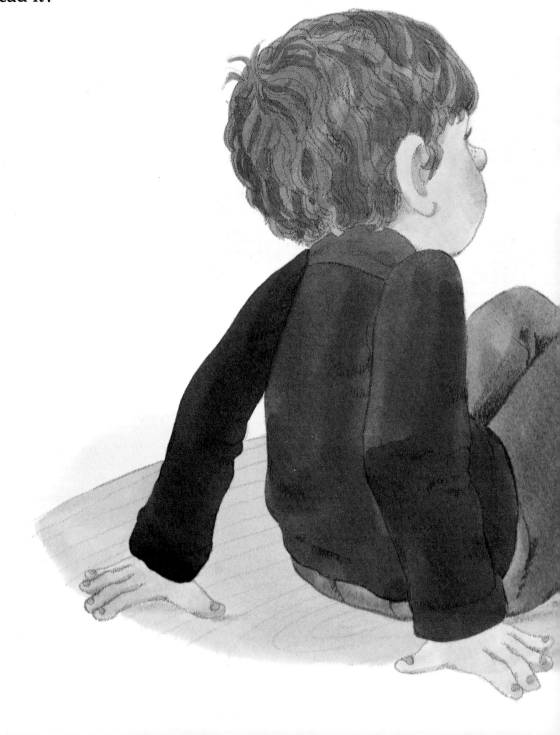

Timothy's eyes lit up. "I sure would!"

"But you couldn't," Friend Bear said sadly. "Right now it wouldn't make any difference to you if the words were upside down like this." Then Friend Bear stood on his head. "And you'll never get to know them if you draw Swamp Monsters when you are supposed to be learning how to read."

Timothy frowned. "I never thought about it that way. Thanks Friend Bear."

He picked Friend Bear up by the leg and straightened him up.

"Oooh!" Friend Bear giggled. "Heavens to fuzzies, that's another ticklish spot!"

"Sorry." But Timothy couldn't resist giving Friend Bear another tickle. Friend Bear giggled. So did Timothy. Then they both laughed louder. Timothy found that he was feeling better.

Later, when they were playing a game, Friend Bear smiled and said, "Timothy, may I ask you a question?"

"Sure, Friend Bear. Go ahead."

"Why do you act silly in school? You know, making faces; teasing."

Timothy was silent for a moment. Then he said, "I'm not sure Friend Bear. Sometimes I wonder if anyone notices me. If they laugh at me, maybe they'll want me for a friend."

"Maybe," said Friend Bear. "But you know, Timothy, it's not hard to have friends. Think about it. If you want somebody to be warm and fuzzy nice to you—"

"You have to be nice to them!" Timothy said.

"Exactly! See if you want to make a friend, you have to be a friend."

"And I guess I shouldn't give them worms," Timothy added.

"Not unless they happen to be worm collectors," Friend Bear smiled.

Before Timothy went to sleep that night, he thought for a long time about what Friend Bear had said.

The next day Mrs. Pratt said, "I have two chickens and you have two chickens. What do we have altogether?"

Timothy almost said, "Lots of eggs," but he didn't. He just pictured four fire engines instead of chickens and raised his hand.

Mrs. Pratt was very pleased.

He didn't draw pictures of Swamp Monsters during reading time, and when Mrs. Pratt called on him, he read every word right.

Mrs. Pratt gave him a dinosaur sticker for his notebook.

On Friday, Timothy started to stick out his tongue
and cross his eyes at Jennifer. Suddenly he remembered
Friend Bear. Instead of making a horrible face,
he smiled.

Jennifer looked surprised for a minute.
Then she smiled back.
Friday was a very good day.

Timothy couldn't wait to tell Friend Bear all about
it. He ran to his room, but Friend Bear wasn't sitting
on Timothy's bed where he usually sat.

Timothy looked
in his closet. He looked
under his bed. He
couldn't find Friend
Bear.

Then Timothy looked on his table. There, looking as bright and sunny as a new day, were two daisies just like the ones on Friend Bear's tummy.

Timothy remembered what Friend Bear had said, ". . . but when you don't need me so much, I'll be on my way."

Timothy picked up the flowers. "Thank you, Friend Bear. I did it. I think I made a new friend."

He wasn't sure, but Timothy thought he heard the daisies giggle.